# COME BACK TO EARTH, ESTHER!

Words and Art by
Josée Bisaillon

NIMBUS
PUBLISHING
NIMBUS.CA

# Esther is an ordinary girl.

Like many other children, she enjoys playing
dodgeball, jumping rope, and daydreaming in
math class. She likes animals and nature,
and she's passionate about chocolate spread.

But what Esther loves
the most, what she
dreams about every
night, is space.

Space, with its magnificent stars,
asteroids, comets, satellites,
and even its black holes.

Esther likes it when people tell her she has her head in the clouds. It makes her think about the immensity of the sky and her biggest wish: to travel on a spaceship, visit the Milky Way, discover constellations, and, of course, walk on the moon.

Esther likes to recreate the solar system
on her plate at dinner.

"Come back to Earth, Esther!" her parents
always say. "Your dinner's getting cold!"

At the dinner table, at school, at the window,
and in bed, Esther spends hours thinking about
the cosmos and the beauty of the sky.

She does not understand
why she should have
to concentrate instead
of daydreaming.
She thinks she can do
both very well.

Every now and then, Esther reads
upside down. It makes her feel like
she's in a spaceship.

While reading her big book about planets for the hundredth time, she wonders, "Could there be a girl on Mars reading a book about Earth?"

The ocean is the perfect place to simulate the effect of weightlessness. When Esther goes to the beach, she floats underwater and imagines herself free, orbiting the Earth.

The rays of light passing through the surface are shooting stars. Occasionally she sees small fish and wonders if, one day, she will meet aliens.

In the evening, Esther's bed becomes a
spaceship setting off to discover distant
galaxies. The northern lights
are spectacular and the cascading stars
are magnificent.

The Earth looks so small,
seen from above.

Esther invents worlds populated by
extraterrestrial creatures, colourful
galaxies, a confetti of shooting
stars, and lush planets.

But above all, she dreams of one thing:
to invent a vehicle that will take her into space.

It's time to get to work!

For several days, Esther searches for materials to build
her spacecraft. She looks in the recycling bin, picks up
old broken toys, walks the forest nearby....

She is very relieved when her parents help her
find the tools she needs.

Today, Esther's room is transformed into a space centre, ready to welcome the new spaceship.

She nails, she glues, she measures.
She cuts, assembles, and adjusts.

She reflects and she tests.

(And she has a snack break—
all this work makes her hungry!)

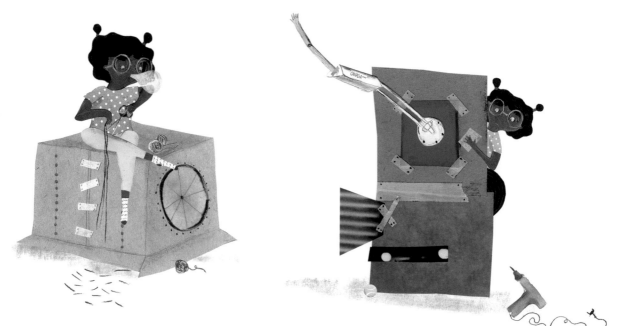

She gets back to work, re-cuts, and readjusts.
She sands a little bit.

And then she paints.

All that's missing now is something special
to wear in space.

Esther gathers a few scraps of fabric, buttons,
thread, and a lot of patience....

And voilà! She crafts the most
amazing spacesuit!

After many tests, the spacecraft is
finally ready to launch....

But takeoff will have to wait until tomorrow.

The next morning, with the help of her parents, Esther prepares the backyard for the big liftoff.

A platform near the maple tree awaits the spaceship and its crew.

Esther's space trip will finally happen tonight!

As the sun sets, everyone gathers to watch the launch of Esther's special spacecraft.

The crew boards the vessel, and the countdown is on...

3, 2, 1...
LIFT OFF!

The spaceship takes off, high in the sky,
leaving behind a dusty cloud as it
reaches for the stars.

It's even more beautiful than Esther
had imagined.

For Henri,
and his thousands of questions
about space.

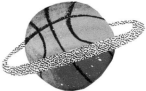

Nimbus Publishing Limited
3660 Strawberry Hill Street, Halifax, NS, B3K 5A9
(902) 455-4286 nimbus.ca

Printed and bound in Canada
NB1479
Editor: Whitney Moran
Design: Heather Bryan

Library and Archives Canada Cataloguing in Publication

Title: Come back to earth, Esther! / art and words by Josée Bisaillon.
Other titles: Reviens sur terre Esther!. English
Names: Bisaillon, Josée, author, illustrator.
Description: Translation of: Reviens sur terre Esther!
Identifiers: Canadiana 20190155523 | ISBN 9781771087841 (hardcover)
Classification: LCC PS8603.I82 R4813 2019 | DDC jC843/.6—dc23

Nimbus Publishing acknowledges the financial support for its publishing activities from the Government of Canada, the Canada Council for the Arts, and from the Province of Nova Scotia. We are pleased to work in partnership with the Province of Nova Scotia to develop and promote our creative industries for the benefit of all Nova Scotians.

  Canada Council for the Arts Conseil des arts du Canada  NOVA SCOTIA